Acting Edition

MU00781054

the way she spoke

by Isaac Gómez

FOR PRODUCTION INQUIRIES

UNITED STATES AND CANADA
info@concordtheatricals.com
1-866-979-0447

UNITED KINGDOM AND EUROPE
licensing@concordtheatricals.co.uk
020-7054-7298

Each title is subject to availability from Concord Theatricals Corp.,
depending upon country of performance. Please be aware that *THE
WAY SHE SPOKE* may not be licensed by Concord Theatricals Corp. in
your territory. Professional and amateur producers should contact the
nearest Concord Theatricals Corp. office or licensing partner to verify
availability.

This work is published by Samuel French, an imprint of Concord Theatricals Corp.

No one shall make any changes in this title(s) for the purpose of production. No part of this book may be reproduced, stored in a retrieval system, scanned, uploaded, or transmitted in any form, by any means, now known or yet to be invented, including mechanical, electronic, digital, photocopying, recording, videotaping, or otherwise, without the prior written permission of the publisher. No one shall share this title(s), or any part of this title(s), through any social media or file hosting websites.

For all inquiries regarding motion picture, television, online/digital and other media rights, please contact Concord Theatricals Corp.

MUSIC AND THIRD-PARTY MATERIALS USE NOTE

Licensees are solely responsible for obtaining formal written permission from copyright owners to use copyrighted music and/or other copyrighted third-party materials (e.g., artworks, logos) in the performance of this play and are strongly cautioned to do so. If no such permission is obtained by the licensee, then the licensee must use only original music and materials that the licensee owns and controls. Licensees are solely responsible and liable for clearances of all third-party copyrighted materials, including without limitation music, and shall indemnify the copyright owners of the play(s) and their licensing agent, Concord Theatricals Corp., against any costs, expenses, losses and liabilities arising from the use of such copyrighted third-party materials by licensees. For music, please contact the appropriate music licensing authority in your territory for the rights to any incidental music.

IMPORTANT BILLING AND CREDIT REQUIREMENTS

If you have obtained performance rights to this title, please refer to your licensing agreement for important billing and credit requirements.

THE WAY SHE SPOKE was first produced by Greenhouse Theater Center (Jacob Harvey, Artistic Director) at Greenhouse Theater Center in Chicago, Illinois on June 20, 2016. The performance was directed by Laura Alcalá Baker, with scenic design by Eleanor Kahn, lighting by Heather Sparling, sound by Sarah Putts, and dramaturgy by Rebecca Adelsheim. The production stage manager was Adia Alli. The cast was as follows:

THE ACTRESS. . . . . Karen Rodriguez

THE WAY SHE SPOKE was produced by Kate Navin, Artistic Producer; Franki De La Vega, Producer; Emilia LaPenta, Producer; and Rachel Sussman, Producer, Off-Broadway by Audible and Baseline Theatrical at the Minetta Lane Theatre in New York, New York on July 8, 2019. The performance was directed by Jo Bonney, with scenic design by Riccardo Hernandez, costumes by Emilio Sosa, hair and makeup by J. Jared Janas, lights by Lap Chi Chu, sound by Elisheba Ittoop, projections by Aaron Rhyne, and vocal coaching by Deborah Hecht. The production stage manager was Evangeline Rose Whitlock, and the assistant stage manager was Alfredo Macias. The cast was as follows:

THE ACTRESS. . . . . Kate Del Castillo

CHARACTERS

THE ACTRESS – Mexican (not Puerto Rican, not Colombian, not Cuban, not Dominican, not Brazilian, not Ecuadorian, not Argentinian, not Chilean, not Guatemalan, not Peruvian, not Salvadorian, not Honduran – she is Mexican. Or of Mexican descent. Or Mexican American. Tejana. Chicana.)

Can be as young as early twenties, and as old as late fifties. She plays fifteen different roles (including herself and the playwright), and every character she embodies is Mexican. So to best ensure that differentiation in inflection, characterization, speech pattern, and physical characterization reflects the breath, depth, and differentiation of Mexican people, THE ACTRESS must be Mexican, or of Mexican descent.

Please cast accordingly.

SETTING

A large, gutted, empty performance space in a big city somewhere.

TIME

Present day.

A NOTE ON STRUCTURE

Because this is a play within a play, there are two forms to note:

OOC (out of character – meaning, THE ACTRESS herself),
and IC (in character – meaning, the CHARACTER she is embodying.)

And there are three layers/journeys to be mindful of:

THE ACTRESS as an independent person, the playwright (whom she both interacts with and plays in the narration of the play within this play), and the world within the play itself (Juárez, the women, the testimonies). Keeping track of the friendship/relationship between the writer and actor is particularly tricky but not necessary.

Additionally, as she dives further and further into the world of the play, the script can slowly disappear from her hands as if she were in the fully-staged production of this play, or in Juárez as Isaac himself. The pages from the script can reappear when she needs to revisit the text, or during moments of intense emotional and mental strain. Vibe this out on its feet. It should feel as though we're not always sure what layer of the play we might be living in, but each layer is always working concurrently.

A NOTE ON NAMES

When THE ACTRESS gets to the names towards the end of the play, there are intentionally more listed than she should read. She should stop when she needs to stop. The audience will be on that journey.

A NOTE ON JOSE LUIS CASTILLO

On page 35 of the script, the playwright notes how long it's been since Esmeralda Castillo Rincon has been missing. Esmeralda has been missing since May 19, 2009. Please update this number each day Esmeralda has been missing throughout the run of the show or until she is found. Thank you.

CONTINUE THE JOURNEY

THE WAY SHE SPOKE is the sister play to *LA RUTA*. I highly recommend reading both. Perhaps consider programming them in rep as these two sister plays are inextricably connected. They speak to each other. Although I wrote *LA RUTA* before *THE WAY SHE SPOKE*, they both speak to ongoing systemic violence against women and femmes in Juárez and beyond; these two plays are two sides of the same coin, illuminating a holistic interrogation and excavation of these women's stories. To this day, I still do not know why the brave and bold women represented in the play you are about to read have trusted me with their stories. I only aspire to be a vessel in hopes that one day, dear reader, one of you might know what to do to stop all this.

For Karen

(A large, gutted, empty performance space in a big city somewhere. Could be a theater. Could be a basement. Could be a storefront. Somewhere performances happen. In between shows, perhaps.)

(A few lights are on, but they're not very bright and they blink on and off – a sign they need to be changed soon.)

(The light from the moon pours inside through a dirty window. Occasionally, a car driving by can be heard, the sound of Reggaeton music* pulsing as it passes by. The sound of rain can be heard from outside. It's pouring. Lightning or thunder, perhaps.)

*(After some time an **ACTRESS** knocks on the door.)*

(Nothing.)

(Then, she knocks again.)

ACTRESS. *(OOC and heard O.S.)* Hello?

(Knocks. She tugs at the door, it opens. Creaky.)

(O.S.) Anybody there?

(She slowly pokes her head inside.)

---

* A license to produce *the way she spoke* does not include a performance license for any third-party or copyrighted music. Licensees should create an original composition or use music in the public domain. For further information, please see the Music and Third Party Materials Use Note on page iii.

Helloooo –

> *(She walks in carrying several tote bags, a big coat, an umbrella – her entire life is with her. Actors. She notices a table with a script on it, waiting for her to thumb through it.)*

Oh.

> *(She slowly walks in, dealing with her wet coat, throwing her things on the table and chair, settling in. She drops something. As she picks it up, she looks out into the audience and gasps like she's just seen a ghost. Sitting there, watching her, is the playwright.)*

Ay me asustaste! What are you doing sitting out there, huh? *Pareces un creep.* You almost gave me a heart attack!

> *(She continues to unpack and settle in. He set up the room for her. That was nice.)*

Sorry if I smell like coffee. I was texting my mom because. Well, I mean you know how she gets when I don't text her like every ten minutes, she swears someone kidnapped me or something. And so I'm texting my mom and I'm not looking where I'm going, right? So I just *ram* into this guy carrying like two trays of iced coffees and of course <u>*my*</u> ass is the one who gets coffee all over, and, – you know what? Can I say something? I'm just gonna say it. Today has been a really (.) shitty (.) day. Okay? I was in a fucking hurry trying to get here from this...<u>*terrible*</u> audition, and you know how long it's been since someone's called me in, right, so I was like, "thank god." But *then* I walk in the room, and I see three guys behind the table... and they're all white. So I was like "hm," right? It's for something on Netflix or Hulu, *o algo así, ya no me recuerdo,* and my character's name was CHA CHA.

So I'm about to do the scene and they're like, "do you have any questions?" And I'm like looking at the script and looking at them and I'm thinking, "should I say something, should I say something."

(Beat. A moment.)

And so I turn to these guys and I say, I tell them, I say, "why does she have to be in lace underwear the whole scene?" And these guys go, "well, her name's Cha Cha." And I go, "Right. But *why*...?" And they go, "because she's got that 'cha cha cha.'"

(Beat. A moment.)

And I'm standing there...
looking at this guy,
looking at my life thinking...
"is this all it's ever gonna be?"
How many times am I gonna have to dye my hair black,
or show up to auditions dressed like a *puta*,
or play maids who don't speak English,
or get called in for characters named Cha Cha,
and I just... I just...
I don't know if I can do it anymore.

(Her phone dings. She checks her text message.)

Ay perdón es mi mamá.

(She takes a moment, texts her back.)

(Texting, reading aloud.) "*Estoy con Issac.*"

(She hits "send." A reply comes back almost immediately. She reads it, smiles.)

(To the playwright.) Que te manda besos.

(Beat. A moment.)

Okayyyyyy...

(She sits down at the table. There's a freshly printed script sitting in front of her, begging for her to open it.)

Alright let's see here...ohhhh it's still warm.

(The playwright doesn't say anything.)

Okay. So don't hate me but... I haven't read it.
I know! I'm sorry! I know should have. But it's not like I had the time, I was in the middle of breakfast when you sent it. I tried to pull it up on my phone on my way over here but then my mom texted, and then the coffee guy and...yeah. I'm sorry.

(Beat. A moment.)

But I'm excited. It's been too long. Remember when we lived in that shitty apartment by that Vietnamese place – you remember the one – and you'd be working on a new play till two, three in the morning and then wake my ass up so you could hear your pages out loud before going to rehearsal? You're like the only writer who *actually* wants to know what I think. And you know how much I love doing this shit for you. It's my bread and cheese, or however you say it.

(Her phone dings.)

(Yelling at her phone.) MAMA! YA!

(She texts her back real quick, turns it off.)

Sorry, sorry. It's off.

(A moment.)

Ora sí.

(She opens the script to the title page. She pronounces "mythologia" as "my-th-o-lo-jai-uh.")

"The Way She Spoke: A Docu-Mythologia –"

(Trying again, phonetically.) Myth-o-<u>lo</u>-gee-uh.
Mytho<u>lo</u>gia.

Ah, okay.

(Trying again, getting it right.) "The Way She Spoke: A
Docu-Mythologia" written by Isaac Gómez.

Watchelaaaaaaa! Docu-mythologia, *guao*, so fancy!

> *(Flips the page.)*

Okay don't need to read that.

> *(Flips the page.)*

Don't need to read that...

> *(Flips the page.)*

Great. Here we go.

> *(A moment.)*

I'm so proud of you, *hermano*.

> *(And then, she begins.)*

> *(IC.)*

It's snowing.
It never snows here.
At the west tip of Texas, the blazing sun melts tar on
the railroad tracks by the Zaragoza Bridge.

> The *paleta* guy wipes his brow from his fifteen-
> hour work day
> > and the road kill in the lower valley emits a
> > familiar scent of...
> > > I don't know.
> > > > Childhood, maybe?

But never snow.

The line at the border crossing
is shorter than I remember it.
But it's been years and everything feels like forever
when you're twelve years old.
Yet it all looks the same.
A city frozen in time.
El Centro, Ciudad Juárez,
and it's snowing.

    So peaceful. So beautiful. For a city riddled with
anger and sorrow and confusion, it's surprisingly calm.
No sign of the kind of violence I remember when I was
twelve.

        Of photos of decapitated heads as a warning
        from the *narcos*,
            or of phone calls from my cousins saying,
            "take the backroads instead,
                it's safer."

None of that this time.
Just quiet...and snow.
You can't see the potholes by her house or mine and
for the first time, it feels like we are all the same.
The thin blanket of white plush hides
    the grit below my feet,
        the lack of sidewalks,
            the missing streetlights,
                the broken down vehicles and the
                run down repainted school busses
                taking women to the factories at all
                hours of the day and night.

    *(She circles "factories" in her script. A note for
    the playwright later. She goes back, and reads
    that again.)*

                the broken down vehicles and the
                run down repainted school busses

taking women to the factories at all hours of the day and night.

For a moment I've forgotten why I'm here but a hush rushes over the busy streets as the sun begins to set and I hear my mother's voice ringing in the forefront of my mind:

"*Mijito por favor.*"

(*OOC.*)

Mijito? No guey it's *mijita*, you know this, it's simple grammar, "*ah,*" "*ah,*" *mijita, porque soy una mujer y tu –*

(*A moment and a realization.*)

Wait...I'm playing you?

(*She laughs.*)

This is gonna be fun. *Ora si,* let me take it back.

(*She takes it back, and makes a slight adjustment now that she knows she is playing the playwright.*)

(*IC.*)

For a moment I've forgotten why I'm here but a hush rushes over the busy streets as the sun begins to set and I hear my mother's voice ringing in the forefront of my mind:

"*Mijito por favor.* Please don't go."
"I have to."
"It's too dangerous."
"I'm the only one who can."
"They're doing just fine."
"No. They're not. "
"This isn't your mess to clean up, let it go."

"I can't."

For years I'd go in and out of Juárez with no cares in the world, and she'd never say anything to me, but despite walking my cousin Karla to the corner store when we were kids,

      despite visiting Juárez less and less when more bodies started hanging from the bridge,

            despite this indescribable feeling in the pit of my gut that something wasn't right,

I never knew the truth about these women.

> *(She circles "I never knew the truth about these women." Important information. Clues to the world that's about to unfold.)*

And that embarrassed me.
Everybody knew it but me.
And the more I read.

      The more I researched.

          The more I became obsessed.

I needed to go back to Juárez and see it for myself.
But I haven't been back since I was a kid.
Would I even know where to go?
What to do?
Who to talk to?
So I got my passport, called my friend Blanca, and next thing you know, I'm here.

> *(The world around us starts to fade. It's almost as if the **ACTRESS** were in Juárez, living this moment as it's happening.)*

And my mother hates me for it.

      And she begs me to be home before dark.

But I don't leave.
I can't.

They won't let me.

The pictures of these women are like shadows.

You don't always notice them, but they follow you wherever you go.

> *"Ayudanos a Localizarla"*
>> *A quien? Esmeralda?*
>>> *Brenda?*
>>>> *Guadalupe?*

You can't walk through *El Centro* without seeing them.

I mean, you can't walk through *El Centro* without seeing a lot of things, but it's like they stare at you, just waiting for you to stop and look...

and there are hundreds of them.

New faces.

> Old faces getting older.

>> Lost girls with no one to find them.

Here's the thing.

"There is no better place in the world to kill a girl than in Juárez."

I read that in a magazine once.

> It made me sick to my stomach because Juárez is my home.

> Okay so I never actually lived on *this* side of the border but my cousins did.

> Every other weekend was spent here...with them.

> *Carne Asadas,*
>> baptisms,
>>> funerals,
>>>> *la pulga* with my *Nini.*

It <u>wasn't</u> home.

But it also was.

Every night when I was a kid, I would climb to the roof of my house in El Paso to look at the stars. And from the tallest point of my rooftop, behind

me were the Franklin mountains and right in front
of me
    – *la Sierra de Juárez.*
Two cities with two mountains hugging the people
between them. And when I looked towards
la Sierra de Juárez, if I stood on my tippy toes,
I could see it:

       The broken houses,
           the Mexican flag,
               the barbed wire fences
            all of it.
               Ciudad Juárez.

A ten minute drive.
A fluidity like Kansas City or Texarkana.
    Closer than the closest Walmart,
           closer than the closest Starbucks,
                closer than...closer than close.

When you live in a border city,
both sister cities are your home.
Your feet are planted in two places at once
and these people know you better than anyone
else in the entire world
because the rest of the country is trying to
pretend like you don't exist.
Like you don't matter.
Like a bridge
or a wall
is enough to say "you are here"
or "you are there"
but when you live in a border city,
you are *everywhere.*
And I haven't been to my sister city since they
found my

uncle dead…
> and naked by the Rio Grande
>> but that's a story for another day.

*(Beat. We're back in the **ACTRESS**'s space.)*

*(The **ACTRESS** looks out. Is this true? She didn't know this.)*

(OOC.)

Is this…did this really happen?
'Cause you told me your uncle Max died of a heart attack so I –
Sorry, you don't have to answer that. I just…
Sorry.

(IC.)

So Juárez.
> I went to my first *quinceañeras* there.
>> I got my first formative haircuts there.
>>> I spoke the little Spanish I know there.

But today: *this* Juárez.
With these women and these pictures
and these streets and lights and pink crosses?
This Juárez is different.
> And in this Juárez…it's snowing.

(And just like that, we are back where we left off.)

> My friend Blanca & I decide to meet by the Zaragoza Bridge.
She & her mom know the area a lot better than I do so they agree to be my guide.

> "You ready?"

"I...think so."

"I'm ready. People don't ask questions around here.
They know what might happen if they do."

We start driving towards the pink crosses,
but I'm more interested in seeing what else I can find
while I'm here.
Will anyone talk to me?
Will I be afraid?
Will I find anything here,
          or worse, will I find nothing at all.

"Here we are. *Campo Algodonero*."
"How many women were found here?"
"Eight. Esmeralda Herrera Monreal,
Laura Berenice Ramos Monárrez,
Claudia Ivette González,
María de los Ángeles Acosta Ramírez,
Mayra Juliana Reyes Solís,
Merlín Elizabeth Rodríguez Sáenz, and
María Rocina Galicia."
"That's seven."
"They couldn't identify the last one.
Her face was mangled from asphyxiation,
her nipples...
     had been bitten off...
          her entire body
               completely destroyed."

*(Beat. She looks out at the playwright and
we're back in the* **ACTRESS***'s space.)*

(She circles this last paragraph.)

(OOC.)

Sorry. That –

Wow. I didn't know that.

I mean I knew about *las desaparecidas,* everyone in *México* does, *pero* I just uh…

I didn't know *that.*

> *(She looks around for something.)*

Let me…let me take it back.

> *(The **ACTRESS** readjusts her performance space perhaps. Takes a note or two in the script – thoughts for the playwright later. She takes a sip of water.)*

I'm gonna take it back.

> *(She walks through her space. She's better on her feet and she knows it.)*

> *(IC.)*

"How many women were found here?"
"Eight. Esmeralda Herrera Monreal,
Laura Berenice Ramos Monárrez,
Claudia Ivette González,
María de los Ángeles Acosta Ramírez,
Mayra Juliana Reyes Solís,
Merlín Elizabeth Rodríguez Sáenz, and
María Rocina Galicia."
"That's seven."
"They couldn't identify the last one. Her face
was mangled from asphyxiation, her nipples
had been bitten off, her entire body
completely destroyed."
"How old were they?"
"The oldest was nineteen."
"And the youngest?"
"Fifteen. Two young boys were playing kickball

and found them here."
"Who did this?"
"Some say it was the police. Some say it was a
gang. I think it was all of the above."

(A moment.)

(And just like that, we're back in Juárez.)

Campo Algodonero is exactly what its name says it is.
A *campo*. *De algodón*. A cotton field.
It's a mouthful, isn't it?
Just trying to say it gives you cotton mouth,
<u>*Campo Algodonero,*</u> *chingado.*
Just like any other.
But unlike every other cotton field in Juárez,
it became a burial site over night.
No one knows *Campo Algodonero* without knowing the
eight women who were found here.
And now it's a memorial.
A statue of a woman
reaching towards the sky with names
of missing women on her dress
keeps them alive.
At least for me.

It's uh…
it's hard to put into words.
Because once you know, you can't <u>*un*</u>-know.
You know?

Anyway.
I stood there for a while.
And stared at the pink crosses before me.
But the one I kept coming back to was
"unidentified." It took my breath away.

As if she were nothing more than the pink cross that
stands in her place.

"No identificada."

I felt a pinch on my elbow.

> "*Ey.* We can't stay too long.
> People get suspicious."
> "Why?"
> "Why do you think?"

I let that sit with me before we are off to the next place.

> *(She circles that last text. Where are we going?*
> *She doesn't know. But she follows it, curiouser*
> *and curiouser.)*

Blanca's mom turns on the radio –

> *Volveré,* K-Paz De La Sierra.

> Sounds like it, anyway.

She smiles and sings along.

> *(Beat. A moment.)*

I want to join her, but I don't.
I look at her eyes in the rear view mirror
and can't help but notice a gleam of thrill as she makes
a left turn into a neighborhood where the houses look
poorer than the ones we passed this morning.
Her bangs bouncing as we drive down roads made of
mud.

>   Her smile growing bigger and bigger
>   the further away from the city center we get.
>   Something about this whole thing feels like
Nancy Drew to her, I think.

> "Where are we going?"
> "I know a woman who lives down the street.

Her daughter is still missing.
Her name is Yoli."
"We're gonna talk to her?"
"*Pues si*. Isn't that why you're here?"
"And – what? We're just gonna be like 'hey girl
sorry about what happened – you wanna talk
about it for this play I'm writing?'"

She slams on the breaks.

"Is this funny to you?
"What? No, of course not."
"'Cause what we're doing isn't funny."
"No, I know. I'm just. I'm nervous. That's all."
"If you're gonna do this, then do it.
No fakies. No backtracks.
These women have been through enough
mierda without *you* rolling around in it. So if you're
gonna do this, do it for real. And do it for them."

I nod my head and we keep driving.
I knew the possibility of meeting and speaking with
these women was pretty high.
But for some reason I didn't think it was actually going
to happen.
What if I say the wrong thing?
Do the wrong thing?
I mean my balls are literally at my throat at this point,
I'm freaking out.
And before I can even ask to turn around...
        we are here.

(And just like that, we're in Yolanda's house.)

At her house.
There are no *cruces* or *virgencitas* around
which surprises me.

Stacks of jeans falling off an ironing board.
And a picture of her daughter
printed on a huge foam board
hanging on her living room wall.
Blanca points out the inscription at the bottom:

>"*Mira*. Brenda Ivonne Ponce Saenz. She was seventeen when she went missing."

Yoli smiles softly.
Her other daughter running around the house, in and out of the yard barefoot and without a coat.
She hugs Blanca's mother
before nodding a "hello" in my direction.
We sit down.

>*(The* **ACTRESS** *pulls up a chair, sits.)*

And then...she speaks:

>*(The* **ACTRESS** *embodies Yoli, a mother in her forties.)*

"I was walking down the street the other day
and I could have sworn I saw her. It couldn't
have been her and I think I knew that while it
was happening, but I stopped this beautiful
girl in the middle of the street and asked,

'*Senorita*...have you seen my daughter? Here
is her picture. She has dark hair and brown
eyes and she was last seen with her friend
looking for a job at *El Centro*...around eleven
or twelve o'clock.
Have you seen her?
She looks just like you.'

I used to dream about her every night.
She would visit me in my sleep and she'd tell me

to never stop looking because someday, one
day, she'd swear I'd find her.
For a while, so did I.
But I haven't dreamt about her in years, and I'm
starting to lose hope that I'll ever see her
again. If I could just have a piece of my
daughter, then I...
You know you can't file a missing person's
report unless they've been missing for seventy-two
hours? Isn't that something.
So I waited.
And waited.
And waited.
I called her cell phone. Over and over again.
No one ever picked up but one day, somebody
answered.
It was a man.
He said he had her.
Mi Brendita.
And that if I give him some money, he'd bring
her back to me... In three years.
But I have nothing to give.
And I told him,
I begged him.
But he hung up the phone.
And no one ever answered again.
A mother's love for her daughter runs deeper
than any *impunidad* in Juárez and I keep my
house the way it is so that she will come home
to me like she used to, hug me like she used
to, and smile at me just the way she used to.
You know nothing's been done. Mm-mm.
Nada. I filed a lawsuit against her friend, but
...there was no proof that she was the one

who took her.
Brenda went looking for a job at a shoe store
in *El Centro* with her friend, and she never came back.
Everything in my gut says
her friend sold her to that man.
I know it was her.
Her friend worked at the *cantinas* down in
El Centro and was always hanging around the
wrong kind of guys.
She left Juárez after the court case. She was
gone for six months, and when she came
back...they killed her.
That was my proof.
When Brenda comes home, I'm not telling the
authorities anything. No.
I'm taking *mi niña* and we will go far away
from Juárez and we'll never look back.
What is this for again?
A play?
Huh.
Can you... Can you pass on a message for me?
For anyone who sees this who might know
where my daughter is?
Where the other daughters might be?
If you have them. Please.
Have pity on the families suffering.
Give them back.
Have pity, and give them back. Please.
I know my Brenda is alive.
I feel it in my bones.
So I will wait for her.
I will wait until she comes back."

*(The world around us fades away, and we're
back in the* **ACTRESS***'s space once more.)*

It wasn't what Yoli said that changed me forever.
It was the way she said it. _Spoke_ it.
    The desperation in her voice
    yet alarmingly calm as if scripted and spoken a
    thousand times before
No tears.
    But a mother grieving all the same.
Why didn't she cry?
I sat there the whole time hearing her words,
    seeing her face,
        and they didn't match.

(OOC.)

Is that a real question here "why didn't she cry?" Or is it
more...? 'Cause it feels pretty obvious to me....

(Beat. A moment.)

But it feels like a really earnest question –
"why didn't she cry?"

*(Beat. She thinks about it but is quick with
an answer without needing much help.)*

Oh! It's *not* about her, it's about you. Got it, got it.
Okay...let's see here...

(She goes back to the script.)

(IC.)

Why didn't she cry?
I sat there the whole time hearing her words,
    seeing her face.
        And they didn't match.

They say burying a child is the worst thing
imaginable. It's unnatural, they say.
Against the order of things, they say.
But what about having to bury a child...
                                with no body to bury?

The snow outside is starting to melt
as the sun hits the high sky. I feel it turn into mush
beneath my tennis shoes.
I don't think anyone can really understand how poor
these people are unless you visit the city and see it
yourself.
These adobe houses are made of one large room with
clothespins and blankets to separate
the living room from the bedrooms from the bathrooms
from the kids' rooms
and on and on it goes.
I take pictures with my disposable camera of the run
down streets and busses passing by,
and I feel a presence
creep slowly towards me.
It's a man.
Older, taut skin, *moreno.*
He never says anything but just inches closer and
closer till I finally step away and am back in the car
with Blanca
and her mom.

> *(In a quickness, we're back in Juárez, in
> the car with Blanca, her mother, and the
> playwright.)*

"Lock the doors. Did you guys see that?"
"*Que?*"
"That man standing next to me. He was
creepy, no?"

"*Ah si.* He's a *sicario.*"
"*Sicario?*"
"A hitman."
"What?!"
"He's a hitman. One of the best in Juárez."
"A hitman."
"Yeah."
"Just walking down the street."
"*Que si guey.*"
"Why didn't you say anything?!"
"What – you wanted me to yell 'quick get in
the car or he'll kill you!'"
"Kind of!"
"*Ay hombre,* <u>everybody</u> knows him."
"Everybody knows he's a hitman and nobody
says anything about it?"
"Why would we?"
"Uh because he's a HIT MAN?!"
"And risk getting our families killed in the
process? *No gracias.*"
Everyone in Juárez knows almost
everything there is to know about these kinds of
things. But I'm told it's best to never say anything
because of what might happen if you do.
So in Juárez, we stay quiet.
And we drive on.

We pull up beside another adobe house. Blanca's mom
tells us to go inside, but decides to wait in the car.

"Your mom isn't coming?"
"Uh...nah. Not this time."
"Everything okay?"
"It's...complicated, *ya.*"

Blanca knocks three times.

Two teenagers wet my cheeks
with ninety-nine cent lip gloss,
six or seven kids run around the house playing tag,
two *viejitas* stay seated in front of the small
television set watching *Carrusel*
– my *abuelita* loved that show –
and they don't blink an eye,
even as we sit down for *cafecitos* and cookies.
Blanca and the others catch up, talk about school, boys,
the usual.
Two little girls stare at me
silently as I sip my *café con leche*
and dip my sugar cookie in it for flavoring.
Blanca finishes her beverage and makes moves.

> "*Hola señoras. Cómo están ustedes, euh?*"
> "…"
>
> *(Beat. A moment.)*
>
> "Carrusel, *ay que lindo*! I love this episode."
> "…"
>
> *(Beat. A moment.)*
>
> "*Disculpe*...is Sandra around?"
>
> *(Beat. A moment.)*
>
> *(Then..)*
>
> "SANDRA! BLANCA'S HERE!"

We are guided into a tiny corner of the home where
Sandra sits in a baggy tank top and basketball shorts
down to her knees, playing on her computer to
pass the time.
She reminds me of my cousin Cora.

> Short hair.

More *macho*
      than most of the men in my family.
She and Blanca hug.
It's definitely tense, and I don't really know why.
Blanca introduces us.
I shake her hand, and sit by the bed.
I learn that Sandra was one of the bus drivers
for the *maquiladoras*.
She drove women to the factories and back.

*(The **ACTRESS** circles this text. A note for later.)*

She closes her laptop

*(The **ACTRESS** sets up her space, sits.)*

Gets real close

(She does.)

And speaks:

*(The **ACTRESS** embodies Sandra, a macha bus driver in her thirties.)*

"Have you ever seen a woman picked up out of thin air right before your very eyes?

(A moment.)

Sorry, didn't mean to scare ya. I've seen some... I've just seen some shit, okay? Shit I don't really wanna get into but Blanca tells me you're a good kid and this is for a good cause so I told her I'd pull through, I said, "listen," I said. "I'll talk to him. But you've gotta show him what's really going on here, not the kind of shit you read in the paper

or see in movies or TV shows but the real shit,
okay?" And she said she would so here I am.

(Beat.)

You know women disappear when they
walk home, don't you? Mhmm. Right when
they get off the bus, *that's* when they disappear.
Three months ago, somebody got off my bus and
disappeared just down the street from where
we are now. I always tell them, I say,
"*Cuidense señoritas, por favor,* walk together,
okay?" Girls want to be dropped off right
in front of their houses, not even a block away,
'cause they're scared. I see them.
When I take them as far as the roads let me go,
I see them literally run for their lives.

(Beat.)

You know those girls, the *maquila* workers, they
ask all the time if they can be dropped off closer
to their houses. But the *maquila* _owners_ don't
want to let that happen 'cause the streets are
owned by rival gangs, you know? So instead,
women working the night shift get dropped off
at a local point where they're picked up
by *las madres* and walk each other home.
The danger hours are the ones really early in the
mornings, or really late at night.
I hate working those shifts. It messes with you,
you know? When the darkness falls. It's so easy.
It's just so easy.

(Beat.)

The busses we drive are called *la ruta.*

We take women to the *maquilas* and back, that's it.
They're not like the other busses that take you
around Juárez, no. Those busses are different,
okay? They're different.

(Beat.)

Just last week, two young girls were
walking to my bus in *El Centro*, right? A car
pulled up right beside them and said "get in
the car" and they started running as fast as they
could. I held my door open and I yelled, I yelled to
them "*Corran! Apurense!* Get inside, *rapido!*"

(A moment.)

Only one of them made it. The other
was found by a dumpster three days later.

(Beat.)

I think of *la ruta* as a machine
to *el Diablo*. The bus that delivers women to
their graves. *Eh, eh!* But the bus I drive is
different, okay? It's not like the other busses, no.
The bus <u>I</u> drive keeps them safe.
Escríbelo."

Sandra quit driving for *la ruta* earlier this week.
She talks about it as if she's out there on the road,
still driving,
          but she's not.
I think a part of her still feels guilty about what
happened, so she stays home and doesn't go anywhere.
          Maybe it's easier.
                    I don't blame her.

(The world of Juárez fades away and we're back in the **ACTRESS**'s *space.)*

(OOC.)

What do you mean, you don't blame her?
Don't you see what she did, she she she saved someone.
She *did* something, and what, she's just gonna quit?
After all that. She's, like, the one person on the other side who actually knows what's going on and has lived to tell it...as a woman...

(The **ACTRESS** *revisits the text again, circles the line.)*

...*I* blame her. I do.

(Beat. Nothing.)

(IC.)

I clock the time.
I smile.
I thank her.
I don't really know what else I'm supposed to do.
I nod to Blanca, and we turn to go.
In the car, we remain silent.

(Silence. A long one. She looks at the playwright to see if he's going to say something. He doesn't. She reads on.)

We round a corner by an industrial looking site.

(The site comes to life.)

"Where are we now?"
"Can't you tell? These are the *maquilas*.
Textiles. Electronics. Chemicals. You know women lose fingers in there sometimes. These

machines are so heavy and they have to work
so fast."
"You think they'll actually let us in?"
"We can try."

We pull up to the RCA *maquila*; one of many owned
and operated by the United States.
Women earn about five dollars and fifty cents
for a twelve-hour workday. There are more than one
million people employed by these factories.
       Most of them young Mexican women.

(The **ACTRESS** *circles the text she just read,
underlines it furiously.)*

We get out of the car and I find myself walking past
pictures of more missing women like the ones from
this morning;
their black and white faces now hauntingly familiar.
Their names ringing in my ears as I read them.
Two men stand at the gate.
Blanca's mom flashes the most generous smile.

  "*Hola señoritos*. My daughter and her friend are
  doing a report for school on economics and
  want to highlight some of the amazing work
  of the *maquilas*.
  Do you think...
  do you think it be okay to let them in just for a
  little peek?"
  "This is for a report?"
  "*Siiiiiiiii.*"
  "For...school?"
  "*Siiiiiiiii.*"
  "Let's see some school identification then."

Blanca and I pull out our college IDs and hand them
to the men.

"UT Austin huh?
What brings you all the way to Juárez?"
"We're from here."
"That so? Hm. One second."

He turns away and speaks into his headset.
I can't quite make out what he's saying until he starts
reading our identification cards, including
our addresses. He turns back to us.

"Can you wait about twenty minutes? The
manager would like to escort you himself."

Blanca's mom pulls our IDs from him,
same smile as before.

"Actually, sorry, but we have to head home.
Muchas gracias, eh."

And just like that, she rushes us back to her car and we
are on the road again.
We never got to look inside the *maquila*.
It was probably for the best.
In Juárez, you have to accept these things
for what they are.
The longer you let it linger,
the more it weighs you down.

(Beat. A moment.)

We pull over at a corner store so Blanca and I can get
some cash for her mom.

She needs to pay some bills while we're out and about.
We step into the store.
Juárez police officers stand firm
at the entrance with their AK-47s.

And there is a group of men gathered in the
corner, laughing and just hanging out.

Blanca tugs at her sweatshirt

> "I need you to stay ten feet away from me."
> "Why?"
> "Just stay ten feet away and just watch. I want
> you to see the way men are here."
> "Blanca I'm not sure this is a good idea."
> "Please. You have to see it to know it. Please."

Blanca wears loose fitting jeans, a hoodie, and a pair of
sneakers. She has no makeup on and her hair is in a
ponytail. She told me before she does this intentionally.
I've never asked why.
As she walks over to the register the men shift their
attention towards her. Something about the way they
look at her –
not necessarily lust, but more like...hunger.

> *"Ey mamacita,"*
>
> *(The* **ACTRESS** *grabs her crotch, thrusting,*
> *embodying the men.)*
>
> "You too good for daddy's dick or what?"

The others put their hands on their waistbands,
showing Blanca their guns.

> "Give us a smile...or we'll rip you to pieces and
> throw you away just like the others."
>
> *(A moment.)*
>
> *(As Blanca, as the* **ACTRESS***, or both.)* "Can you
> come here, please."

I rush over and the men...

walk away.

Slow.
Pissed.

Their eyes
locked with mine.
I think they thought she belonged to me.
Not in the way you think like if we were dating,
     which is still fucked up because no one should
     "belong" to anyone,
but as if I were her *dueño*. Her owner.
Because I am a man.

    "Blanca, that was so dangerous, why did you
    do that?"
    "Because you needed to know. And now you
    do."

But do I?
Do I somehow so suddenly know what this is like?
What it feels like, what it looks like, the taste in your
mouth when it's happening or the lump in the back of
your throat when it's over?
I don't know if that's true.
I don't think it will ever be true.

    (Beat. The **ACTRESS** *looks at the playwright.*
    Of course it will never be true.)

On the way back to the car, Blanca tells me what the
deal is with Sandra, the bus driver from before.
It turns out Sandra used to date Blanca's older sister,
Lilian. Blanca's parents didn't take this very well,
which is what ultimately split them apart.
Blanca's sister is now married.

    To a man.

    (The **ACTRESS** *sets up her space, her*
    circumstances, her character. She's gotten
    quite good at this.)

    And just like that,

I'm sitting right beside Lilian in her home.
Las Virgencitas staring at me from every
wall space I can see.
They're pretty. They remind me of home.

*(The **ACTRESS** embodies Lilian, a naca*
frescita *in her thirties.)*

"*Ay pues...* I've never taken out the trash by
myself. My whole life, I always had someone
do it with me. My father, my brother, and now
my husband. It's so dangerous here for a
woman we can't even take out our own
garbage, can you believe that?

 (Beat.)

I worked at the *maquila* too. Mhmm *con mi*
mama before Blanca was born.
Ay, the environment there was so tense.
Mostly women. Hardly any men. Lots of precaution.
Always.
"Don't walk in the middle of the road.
Walk against traffic so you're aware at
all times. Walk in groups especially at night."
I worked too close to home to take *la ruta* so we
were always walking. But you see, you can't
really trust the bus drivers either, no.
No, no, no. You see the bus drivers always end up
raping the last girl on the bus. It's typical.
It happens. A lot of girls fall asleep on the busses
on the way home and then WHAM!
It's over.

 (Beat.)

In *El Centro*, if a car comes to you
asking you for directions, as soon as you get

close they will take you. Girls in this area
would go to *El Centro* for shopping or work or
whatever and a lot of the time, that's where they
disappear.
Being alone here as a woman makes you feel
afraid and vulnerable and you just know it's
not a good idea to be alone. We have to look
out for each other. *Mira.*

*(She pulls out a newspaper headlining
Marisela Escobedo Ortiz.)*

This is Marisela Escobedo Ortiz. She is a mother
who's daughter Rubí went missing for some time.
When they found her, she was chopped up and
burned in a dumpster.
She was killed by her boyfriend.
They lived together and had a kid.
Marisela wanted justice for what happened to
Rubí but it never happened.
He was acquitted of all charges
even though there was proof he did it,
he confessed! So she decided to take matters into
her own hands, and she became an activist.
She went marching,
        from Juárez to Chihuahua,
               267 miles, to demand justice.
And when she got to the municipal court
on December 16, 2010?
They killed her.
Shot her dead right
there.

(Beat. A moment.)

Isn't that messed up?

(*Beat.*)

You noticed all my *virgencitas*, huh?
All over the house. You like? You can keep one if
you want. *Ah no?*

(*Beat.*)

Bueno.

(*Beat.*)

Eh? No, no, no, no you've got it all
wrong. *La virgencita* isn't significant to *las
mujeres de Juárez*. She's significant to <u>*las madres
de Juárez*</u>. She listens. Because she is a mother
who has lost, too."

(*Shift.*)

I couldn't get the image of Marisela out of my head.
Lilian tells me she marched naked,
      barefoot,
         nothing more than
her daughter's image on a poster board around her neck.
267 miles from Juárez to Chihuahua...

Did she walk at night?
    Did she march alone?
        Why were they so threatened by this one
        woman?

I try to look up videos of her on my phone...
but there's nothing.
    Why?
I scroll through YouTube.
Click: Hundreds of women marching through
downtown Juárez
    Click: Sisters telling stories of missing sisters and
    empty bedrooms

Click: Fathers finding bones of their daughters
in the desert
Click: One father.
Thousands of views.

*(The world slips away and we're back in
Juárez.)*

Jose Luis Castillo. His daughter Esmeralda has been
missing for 4,258 days.
She was last seen in *El Centro* waiting for the bus,
and Jose Luis has been marching,
protesting,
berating government officials ever since for
their inaction.

(Beat. A moment.)

Sometimes...they deliver bags of bones
to parents of lost girls hoping that'll shut
them up.
Most of the time, those aren't even their
bones, but someone else's.

I hit replay on his video over and over again.
I can't take my eyes off him.
Something about the way he wears Esmeralda's picture
on his jacket like armor as he appeals
to guards standing between him and
El Presidente Mexicano, Enrique Peña Nieto
on a rare visit to Juárez.
There's writing on the bottom of her picture.
It reads, "Don't forget me. I'm still missing."

*(The **ACTRESS** embodies Jose Luis Castillo, a
father and an activist in his fifties.)*

*Quiero justicia. Que busque a mija. Esta bien eso?
Que salgan sus malos y le siguen "saquenlo,*

arrestenlo, chigenselo" y verán ustedes como me
arrastaron, ustedes mismos. Señores ustedes tienen
hija, ustedes tienen mama, ustedes tienen madre!
Si tuvieran una hija desaparecida, que haría?
Digame, que haría? No haría todo lo que yo hago?
Me vale madre que me hayan arrastrado y me vale
madre que me haigan golpeado! Yo voy estar aquí.
Voy a seguir haciendo exigencias porque cumplan
con su trabajo.

No que los mandan a golpearnos, no que nos
mandan a reprimirnos. Señores, yo no estoy aquí
por gusto, estoy aquí por necesidad – porque quiero
encontrar a mi hija. Yo no quiero una pinche
televisión. Yo quiero mi hija de corazón. Es lo que
quiero y es lo que vengo a exigirle.

Este cabrón estan comiendo a dentro muy a gusto.
Y yo, donde esta mi hija? Donde esta mi niña?

(Beat. A moment.)

I feel like I've heard that question a million times today:
"Where is my daughter?"
Such a simple question with no easy answers.
No answers...but here's a brand new television instead,
like are you fucking kidding me?

A television set in exchange for his silence.
A television set to make it all go away.
A television set instead of his daughter.

People don't just disappear
without somebody noticing,
"Where is my daughter?"
The silent response from the police,
    from the government,
        from the church,
            from the newspapers,

from the factories,
from the *narcos,*
from the bus drivers is an
answer in and of itself:
it's not just one thing, it's *everything.*
Intertwined.
Interworking to keep things quiet,
keep people quiet
because their silence will protect them
while the women around them show up dead.
"Where is my daughter?"
Do you know where she is?
Do you?
Do you?
Do you? Do you? Do you?

(She takes it to the sky.)

Do you, *Virgencita?*
You're seeing this, right?
You're watching this whole thing play out?
Your pictures are everywhere
but you've never felt further away.

Are you there?
They need you.
I need you.

(Her eyes stay fixed at the heavens for a moment. Maybe a moment too long. Nothing.)

Forget it.
Don't know why I even bother.

(In a quickness, something shifts. A cacophony of prayer, in English, in Spanish, in Spanglish, young voices, old voices, lost

voices, found voices — but all of them women,
can be heard. It's deafening. The **ACTRESS**
covers her ears. It's painful.)

(The sky slowly breaks open like the sun
bursting through clouds after forty days and
nights of flooding, or the resurrection of a
murdered child.)

(The sound crescendos to a haunting and
abrupt stop and like a possession or an
apparition, the **ACTRESS** *becomes* la virgen
herself. And in this, she presents less like a
deity and more like you and me. Ageless.
Timeless. Casual, almost.)

Shhh.

(She talks directly to the playwright. Or the
audience. Or both.)

Hi.
Can you hear them?
Sorry, I know it can get a little...

(She does an awkward hand gesture voice
combo to finish this thought.)

You get used to it, though.
I hear them all the time.
After two thousand years
it just sort of...yeah. You get the picture.

(Beat. A moment.)

Do you know what it's like...
        to have a million voicemails
            but your voicemail box
    never gets full?
That's what it's like in my head.

Except every voicemail
    is being played
        at the exact same time
and it feels like
    hundreds
    of thousands
        of millions
    of people
are yelling at me,
    crying for me,
        praying to me,
from every possible direction:
    "*Por favor, Virgencita, cuidela.*"
    "*Virgen*, bring my daughter back to me."
    "*Dónde estás, Virgencita?*"
I get that last one a lot.
But I can't get to all of them.
It's impossible, there are too many.
And it kills me.
    It kills me.
        It does.
So what's the point then, right?
Why do they keep praying
        hoping
    when nine times out of ten nothing happens?
That's a good question.
Except...something *does* happen. I listen.
And even if they can never hear me, they feel me.
    Even though they never see me,
        they know I'm there,
            holding their hands,
                wiping their tears,
    always a constant presence.

Because for *las mujeres de Juárez,*
it's *not* about the nine out of ten.
    It's about the one.
It might just be one,
but that one time out of ten,
means there will be one again,
    and one again,
        and one again,
            and one again,
and don't get me wrong. It's not fair,
    and it's fucked up.
        One out of ten will <u>*never*</u> be enough.
        But that is *my* cross to carry. <u>*Mine.*</u>

    (Beat. A moment.)

    (The wind blows.)

Shhhhhh. Do you hear them?

    (A long moment.)

    (Silence.)

    *(Only the **ACTRESS** can hear them now, the audience can no longer. It's deafening. It's painful. Not in a bad way like she can't take it anymore. But in the way anyone would feel when the responsibility is yours and yours alone.)*

    *(Then, the sound in her mind comes to an abrupt stop and the **ACTRESS** is back in her space, the lights are still dim, the audience now a distant memory.)*

That's how she sounds in my head, anyway.
I don't know. I'm probably wrong.

It's hard to believe that "listening" is enough when women are taken from busses and left in dumpsters.

It's hard to believe that "listening" is enough when nipples of women are worn around the necks of men as dog tags.

It's hard to believe that "listening" is enough
when Brenda is still missing.

Yoli. Still. Waiting.

My thoughts are interrupted as Lilian's husband enters their small adobe home and introduces himself.

He is joined by another man.

Their neighbor.

His name is Celso.

He wears a rosary around his neck and twirls it with his dirty fingers. He was formally convicted of...

murdering...

the eight women found in *Campo Algodonero*.

And he wants to speak with me about it:

> (The **ACTRESS** *looks at the playwright for a moment.*)

> (Then: *she concedes and embodies Celso, a twisted ex-convict in his fiftiess.*)

"You look scared. Don't be scared, *hombre*. I'm harmless. I mean, come on, they let me go, right?

> (He *laughs hysterically at his own joke.*)

Look, kid – you're a kid,
right? How old are you? This is for something you're working on? A report or something? You want the truth? Here it is. Most of these young girls were killed by the police. Plain

and simple. If you go to one of the empty
fields where they turn up and you're there
alone, the police will get you. *Lote Bravo,
Campo Algodonero, todos.* We see police in
these open fields at all hours of the night and
we don't suspect them of doing anything.
What are the police doing in these open
spaces? Why do they look so suspicious?
I mean, come on.
Put two and two together, okay?

(A moment.)

I had a ranch, you know. Yup a ranch
with little animals and everything.
I think I miss that the most. They took
everything I had when they took me in. You
know the fucked up thing about this whole
thing? Is right before they picked me up, they
said they had the murderers of those
women in jail already! They had arrested that
Egyptian *Sharif* and that was that! So if it
wasn't him, and it sure as hell ain't me, then
who did it? Who is doing it?

(A moment.)

After some time, they had to let me go. Not enough
proof. They kept *Sharif* for other reasons but
then arrested *"El Cerillo"* and *"La Foca."* And then
Los Rebeldes after that. And now I hear they're
looking into *Los Aztecas* but those gangs didn't do
it either.
Or maybe they did. I don't know. I wasn't there.

(He laughs at his own joke.)

(Beat. Moment.)

I used to be a bus driver. Yeaup. Yeaup.
I was driving *la ruta* when they pulled me over
and arrested me, fucking pigs. Check this.
I was doing my last route around four or five a.m.,
there were no more women on my bus and
they just pull me over and take me in,
just (.) like (.) that.
No word about it or anything.
Three and a half years wasted in *el cereso,*
that fucking jail house, until they
randomly released me without an apology
or explanation or anything. And THEN they took
me back in for ten days and made me pay
them 10,000 *pesos* before they could let me
go! Can you believe that shit?

(Beat.)

You wanna know my opinion? A lot of
the girls they are finding are victims of *narco*
trafficking. Mhmm. Rival gangs trying to get
even with each other by fucking and killing
their girls. Easy as pie, kid. Easy as apple pie.

(Beat.)

Where else have I worked? Uh. Well.
I worked at a police checkpoint for a while.

(A moment.)

Where?

(Slight grin.)

Campo Algodonero."

(OOC.)

You're fucking kidding me, right?
Well what did you do, did you call the police?
I mean you wrote it right here. "He has a slight grin"
right before he says – "*Campo Algodonero.*"
That's as good a confession as any, right?
RIGHT?!

(No response.)

Okay let me get this straight...
He says they're being killed by the POLICE but
he just HAPPENED to be working at A POLICE
CHECKPOINT where eight women just HAPPENED
to show up dead and and and and and what –?!

*(She doesn't wait for a response and instead
goes back to the text, furiously, desperate
for answers. She breathes heavy and starts
having a panic attack while reading. She and
the playwright have become one.)*

(IC.)

I rush out of my conversation with Celso and my face is
greeted by the sharp winter breeze,
as the sun begins to set.
I hear my mother's voice in the back of my mind,
"*Mijito, por favor, no vayas*, it's too dangerous."
The sun is setting and I *know* I need to leave but I don't.
I can't. They won't let me. The pictures of these women,
they're like shadows, they follow you wherever you go,
there are *hundreds of them*.
It's snowing.
It never snows here.
Why am I so obsessed with the fact that it's snowing?

Where am I?

Where am I going?

Why can't I breathe?

I need to throw up I need to throw up I need to
throw up.

(The **ACTRESS** *needs to throw up.)*

I begin to remember, recollect, reimagine all the things
I've seen, the stories I've heard, and I can't get them out
of my head. It all feels bigger than me all of a sudden.
I mean, the Editor-in-Chief of *El Diaro* wouldn't let me
see their archives for fuck's sake. WHY?

(The **ACTRESS** *becomes the Editor-in-Chief.)*

"*Pinche gringo.*

People aren't walking around Juárez looking over
their shoulders
anymore. No one is scared. More men are killed
than women, don't you know that? This...what do
they call it? Feminicide? It's not real.
This isn't real."

But I was there.

I saw it

I felt it

I know it's real.

The things they know,

the way they know it,

the way they live it,

the way it *lives* within them,

because *ONCE YOU KNOW* YOU CAN'T
UN-KNOW.

(Beat. A moment.)

*(The **ACTRESS** catches her breath. She feels the harsh winter air in Juárez enter her lungs as if she were there herself.)*

I'm standing in the snow in *El Centro*.
The pink crosses with names of women are more familiar now than they've ever been.
Each of them with a story.
All of them worse than the one before:

(She turns the page and sees what's on it. There's no way this is the next part of the story. No way. Absolutely not. She peeks on the next page. And the next. She looks out at the playwright.)

(Beat. A moment.)

(Then, she pulls up the chair and sits, just how she was when she first got there. She takes a deep breath, takes the last beat again, and she reads on. Maybe it starts to snow. It probably does.)

I'm standing in the snow in *El Centro*.
The pink crosses with names of women are more familiar now than they've ever been.
Each of them with a story.
All of them worse than the one before:
Cristina Escobar González, twenty-five years old, beaten to death and found in a car trunk.
Isabel Cabanillas de la Torre, twenty-six years old, shot twice from a high-calibre revolver while riding her bike home from a bar.
Once in the chest. Once in the head.
Unidentified woman, age unknown, found severely tortured and wrapped in a blanket in the working-class Oriente neighborhood.

Lorenza Veronica Calderon, thirty-two years old,
strangled to death and buried in the backyard
of her Juárez home.
Verónica Ruiz, thirty-two years old, raped and brutally
beaten, found lying face down in a puddle.
Teresa Torbellin, thirty-three years old, a factory worker
beaten to death. Her bloody body was dragged
through bushes and dumped in an isolated area.
Guadalupe Santos Gómez, thirty-six years old,
strangled partially stripped, dumped on
wasteland on the outskirts of town.
Lorenza Clara Marie Torres, twenty-six years old,
killed, burned, and buried.
Cynthia Irasema Ramos, twenty-one years old, raped
and strangled to death minutes before her
body was found on a sidewalk near a busy
intersection in downtown Juárez.
Alma Brisa Molina, thirty-four years old, a factory
worker, raped and strangled to death.
María de la Luz Martínez García, three years old,
raped, brutally beaten with symptoms of
malnutrition, trauma, and cranial damage.
Unidentified woman, age unknown, executed
by gunfire in her SUV and then set on fire.
Maria Rodriguez, thirty-two years old, stabbed to death
before being buried by her husband in a nearby lot.
Dana Lizeth Lozano Chavez, eighteen years old, found
with her throat slashed at a park next to the Juárez
university. She was four to six weeks pregnant,
and was killed by her jealous ex-boyfriend.
Lidia Elías Granados, fifty-two years old, strangled
and dumped in a garbage can.
Victoria Shawn Iona Anne Marsbergen,

twenty-one years old,
found inside the Colinas de Juárez cemetery
after being beaten in the face with a rock.
Flor Fabiola Ferrer Rivera, twenty years old,
raped, stabbed and strangled to death. She had
been dead for several days before she was
found by co-workers at the restaurant where
she worked, who were worried because she
had not been to work in several days.
Luísa Rocío Chávez Chávez, fourteen years old,
raped and strangled to death. Her body was
found partially clothed.
Sandra Ríos Salmón, fifteen yeears old, raped
and beaten to death; her body was found
in a construction site in the south of the city.
Martha Lizbeth Hernández Moreno, sixteen years old,
raped and strangled to death.
Her body was found in a parking lot.
Lea Gómez Sable, nineteen years old,
brutally beaten and stabbed in front of her
three daughters.
Perla Amaro, thirty-one years old, waited for an Uber
to take her to work at a *maquiladora* when
the driver arrived and shot her in the face.
Juana Cueto López, ninety-one years old, sexually
assaulted and strangled in her home during an
attempted robbery.
Twenty-one young women,
between fifteen and twenty-one years old,
found discarded in a dry stream bed called
Arroyo del Navajo, eighty miles southeast of
the city in the Juárez Valley.
Margarita Cardoza Carrasco,

seventy-four years old, and
Luisa Lorena Hernández Carrasco,
twenty-seven years old,
found dead in their home with their
hands and feet tied.
Unidentified woman, between thirty and
forty years old, found in an abandoned lot near the
international airport of Ciudad Juárez.
She was half-naked, had signs of sexual
assault, and had been strangled. The body had
been thrown out from a moving vehicle.
Reyna Ortiz Rivera, thirteen years old, murdered by
her fourteen year old boyfriend.
Tomasa Herrera Franco, seventy-three years old,
found in the patio suspended from a white electric cord.
Barbara Jazari Batalla Alvarado, three years old,
found on a patio, her arms and legs found
down the street.
Unidentified woman, age unknown, murdered
and found in an empty lot, south of the city center.
Mayra Carbajal Solorio, eighteen years old, sexually
assaulted and her breasts severed.
Died due to excess fluid in her lungs.
Veronica Vega, thirty years old, signs of being
beaten and cut with sharp objects.
Verónica Manchua Molina, thirty-two years old, found
with stab wounds in the abdomen and thorax.
Her husband confessed to having killed her
out of jealousy.
Blanca Guadalupe Sánchez Villalobos, thirty-two
years old, found nude with a red shirt
wrapped around her neck, bruises on her face,
sexually assaulted with a foreign object

and choked to death.

Cecilia Lagarda Amapa, eight years old, raped and
died of her injuries seven days later. Cecilia had
not told her parents about what had happened
to her, and they stated that the only thing that
seemed wrong with her was that she had a
fever and seemed sad.

Perla Esmeralda García Rodríguez, twenty-three years
old, strangled by her ex-husband.

María Antonieta Andazola, thirty-four years old, shot
to death by her husband.

Alejandra Yanel Díaz Sánchez, thirteen years old,
tortured and killed while her mother was
working at the *maquiladoras*.

María Hilaria Pérez Diego, thirty years old,
found in an open field days after her death,
unclothed from the waist down.

Unidentified woman, age unknown, found
burned up to seventy percent in the interior of an
abandoned home.

Unidentified woman, between twenty and
twenty-one years old, found with stab wounds in her
face, neck, chest, back and arms.

Unidentified woman, between twenty to twenty-five
years old, found wrapped in a blanket and put
inside a plastic bag, with signs of extreme
violence by knife in the back, chest and neck.

Bany Rodríguez Ortega, forty-two years old, killed
from multiple gunshot wounds to the head
and chest by a man using an AK-47 rifle.

Dolores Jasso Arias, sixty-five years old, killed by
her son with a hammer and had signs of
external violence all over her body.

Unidentified woman, approximately twenty-thirty
years old, found with multiple wounds and
broken bones, her lifeless body thrown from a
moving vehicle and run over more than once.
Claudia Rodríguez López, thirty years old, shot
and killed while getting into her car.
Alicia Nava Barajas, forty-six years old, strangled by
her twenty-three-year-old son, her body found with her
arms and legs cut off.
Alejandra Díaz Sánchez, thirteen years old, found
inside her home in Ciudad Juárez.
She had been raped and beheaded.
Unidentified woman, thirty-five years old, found dead,
semi-naked, with a strap around her neck.
Claudia Flores Javier, seventeen years old, found in
her home after being raped by three men
while one man hit her several times on the
head with a blunt object.
Elsa Agláe Jurado Torres, twenty-three years old, found
burned with gasoline.
Unidentified woman between forty and forty-five
years old, found with her body swollen
from her wounds with cotton inside
her mouth. It was determined that she
had been beaten and then strangled.
Maria de la Luz Pérez González, twenty-eight years old,
found under a bridge sexually assaulted and
beaten to death.
María Liliana Acosta, nineteen years old,
shot in the throat.
Manuela Cano Luna, forty years old, shot to
death while she was teaching an aerobics class.
Patricia Montelongo de la O, thirty-three years old,

found stabbed multiple times, her body
wrapped in a blanket, tied up, and left in an
empty lot.
Rocío Paola Marin, nineteen years old, found in an
irrigation ditch. She had been raped, tortured
and stabbed more than fifteen times in the back,
stomach, and neck.
Airis Estrella Enríquez, seven years old, found in a
cement-filled drum on a highway on the
outskirts of Ciudad Juárez. She had been
brutally raped and killed.
Anhai Orozco Lerman, ten years old, raped
and strangled to death in her home.
Marta Alicia Meraz Ramírez, forty years old,
shot twice by gang members
while talking to a friend.
Angélica Isabel Pedroza Hernández, twenty-three years
old, found on a dirt road on the outskirts of
Ciudad Juárez. She had been sexually
assaulted, strangled and beaten to death.
Lorenza Veronica Calderon, thirty-two years old,
strangled to death by her husband and found
buried in the backyard of her home.

> *(At some point throughout the reading of the
> names, the* **ACTRESS** *starts to lose it – she is
> emotionally and mentally overwhelmed
> by this entire experience. A mixture of an
> inability to breathe, and a desperation to
> throw up. Maybe she breaks down into tears.
> She is sick to her stomach. She puts down her
> script.)*

> *(The greatest personal cost.)*

> *(OOC.)*

Oh my god...*no puedo...no puedo.*
It's fucked up. It's fucked up.
How long does this go on for?

> *(She flips and tosses through the pages of the script furiously.)*

Huh? Huh?!

> *(She tosses and flips until she gets to the very end. There are hundreds of pages still left to read.)*

> *(She looks back out at the playwright. Disbelief.)*

> *(Beat. A moment.)*

...why don't you come up here and read them yourself?

> *(No response. She waits for a moment.)*

> *(Then.)*

Yeah.

> *(Beat. A moment.)*

Yeah.

> *(Beat. A moment.)*

Okay.

> *(Then, she grabs a page of names from the many scattered across the table. Scraping herself off the ground in whatever way she can.)*

> *(Beat. A moment.)*

Okay.

*(She's determined to finish. She will finish.
She skims the words on this one page. Can
she go on? She wants to. But she can't. It's
insurmountable.)*

Actually...
Yeah I can't do this anymore.
I'm uh...yeah. I'm done.

(She packs up her belongings.)

(Beat. A moment.)

(A moment of this as she gathers her things.)

(But then...she stops.)

Can I ask you a question?

(She takes a breath. This is hard.)

Did it ever cross your mind...
what this would do to me?

(Beat. A moment.)

Because you needed a woman's voice to hear them.
Right?
To hear her,
     and her and her,
          and her, the way
they said it.
The way she spoke it, so *you* get to hear what you need
to hear. But what about me? What about them?

(Beat. A moment. No response.)

It's not only happening in Juárez, you know.
It's happening _everywhere_.

(She heads for the door. Stops. Turns around and takes it all in. Pages of the script scattered all over the floor. The chair on the other side of her room. A part of herself is left here, forever.)

(She looks back out at the playwright.)

(Genuine. Quiet. But hard.) Did you get what you needed?

(She waits a moment for an answer.)

(There is none.)

(And just like that, she's gone.)

end of play

CPSIA information can be obtained
at www.ICGtesting.com
Printed in the USA
LVHW021217280423
745515LV00003B/331